On the

Four stories

Scottish Book Trust

First published in 2007 in Great Britain by
Scottish Book Trust, Sandeman House, Trunk's Close,
55 High Street, Edinburgh EH1 1SR
Sponsored by Standard Life and in association with
Learning and Teaching Scotland

ISBN 978 1 901077 216

Typeset by GreenGate Publishing, Tonbridge, Kent
Printed by Norhaven, Viborg, Denmark

Contents

Down the Pan

by Theresa Breslin

The toilet sat there in the school entrance hall.

A great big lavatory pan. Beside the glass cabinet with the silver cups and shiny award shields. Right in front of the Head Teacher's door.

I saw it as soon as I came into school and I *knew* that it would be my class that would get the blame.

But it wasn't our fault. I mean it was our idea, sort of. But it shouldn't have been us that got ticked off because someone had plonked it down just where the Head would trip over it on the day the school inspectors were due to arrive. We weren't responsible. Definitely not. Our teacher is the one who should have carried the can. Mr Walker is his name, and he's a nutter.

Before I had time to dodge round the corner the Head's door opened and she came rushing out. She was carrying a huge pile of papers and was trying to write something on the top sheet and talk on her mobile at the same time. She didn't see the toilet. And to be fair, if you were a Head Teacher it's not the sort of thing you'd expect to find outside your door first thing on a Monday morning.

There was the most terrific clatter, and the Head went flying amongst a blizzard of white paper.

I managed to catch her mobile phone. I was quite pleased about this as my eye to hand co-ordination skills aren't usually very good.

But did she thank me?

She did not.

'Jamie Macbeth!' She screeched up at me from where she lay sprawled across the toilet pan. 'Why is it always you, or one of your classmates, that are hanging around when something goes wrong in this school?'

In my six years of primary school I've discovered that it's better not to answer questions like that, so I said nothing.

The Head stretched out and snatched her mobile phone from my hand. Not a word of appreciation to me for saving it from being smashed on the floor.

'Would you have any clue at all as to why there is a toilet outside my office door?' she demanded.

'Well yes,' I had to reply to this. 'I think I might.'

Last Friday afternoon our teacher, Mr Walker, had held a Brain-Busting session to help us think up a good idea for the class Charitable Cause Campaign.

Every year in our school, while the Primary Sevens do an Enterprise Project, the Primary Sixes have to choose a Charitable Cause and find a way of raising money for it. Both classes were having bother deciding what their project would be.

4

Heather, who sits next to me, suggested a Sponsored Silence.

'Don't tempt me.' Mr Walker gave us one of his manic grins. 'I'd pay money myself, tons of it, to get you lot to be quiet for a few hours, but we must try to avoid doing the same old things that bore people.'

'Sponsored Spell?' said Ben.

'Boring.' Mr Walker yawned loudly. 'Boring. Boring. Boring.'

'Sponsored Sitting Still?' said Salikah.

'*More* boring,' said Mr Walker, making snoring sounds.

'Sponsored Sleepover?' said Martin.

'*Most* boring.' Mr Walker held his hand up. 'I forbid anyone to use the word "sponsored" again. Why don't you think of the Charitable Cause first? Decide what you want to collect money for. That might help you work out how you actually do it.' He looked at his watch. 'There are three and a half minutes left before the final bell. Do you really want to be here over the weekend? No? Well, think of a good cause. Now!'

It was then that something I'd read on the Internet came into my head. We'd been doing research about water. There's masses of water in Scotland, mainly because it rains quite a lot and that fills up the lochs and rivers and reservoirs. But some countries have hardly any. And the stuff they do have is hard to find.

The people have to dig wells and walk for hours each day carrying it home in jugs and pots. I'd been trawling and clicking and had come across a school in Africa that had found a water source nearby but didn't have enough money to build themselves a toilet.

My hand shot up. 'A toilet,' I said.

Mr Walker shook his head. 'No, Jamie, unless your need is very urgent, you may not go to the toilet.'

'Not *me*,' I said. '*I* don't need the toilet. But there's a school in Africa that does.'

And I explained about the school that had no toilet.

'Yechh!' said Heather, holding her nose. 'Can you imagine that?'

'I'd rather not,' said Salikah.

'Maybe we could collect enough money to build them one?' I said.

'Let's have a show of hands of those who vote for Jamie's suggestion,' said Mr Walker.

With 30 seconds to go before the last bell everyone stuck their hands up.

'Excellent!' Mr Walker thrust his own hand in the air. 'That's it decided. No back backers, you can't change your minds. The school in Africa will have a toilet. Next week we'll discuss the best way to raise funds.' He paused, and a mad light came into his eyes. 'There's this friend of mine who is a builder. I think I'll pay him a visit tomorrow. I might be able

to obtain an eye-catching prop to help Primary Six plan their Charitable Cause Campaign in a non-boring way.' He beamed at me. 'Well done, Jamie! A gold star for you, my lad.'

Six years I've been in primary school and I've never once been given a gold star. I felt brilliant all weekend.

***

I wasn't feeling so brilliant now as the Head stared at me from her seat on the great white throne.

'I'm waiting, Jamie,' she said. 'Please explain to me why there is a toilet—,' she broke off, stared past me at the front door, and scrambled to her feet. 'I can see the school inspectors outside,' she hissed. 'I'll stall them. You find the janitor and have that thing removed. At once!'

Which is how I, helped by the jannie, came to be lugging a huge lavvy pan down the corridor to my classroom.

The Primary Sevens were lined up outside their classroom door waiting for their teacher, and I had to walk past them. At that moment I'd have given back my gold star to avoid the barrage of rude remarks.

'Yo! It's boggin' Macbeth!'

'How's it going? Or have you been already?'

'You're supposed to be toilet trained before you come to school.'

And loads of other rotten remarks.

Most of my class were already inside and sitting down. Mr Walker looked up from his desk as the jannie and I staggered into the class.

'Please don't bring that toilet in here,' he said, getting to his feet. 'It's an important prop in the Charitable Cause Campaign that Primary Six is planning. I want it positioned in the entrance hall for maximum effect.'

'You've already *had* maximum effect,' the jannie told my teacher. 'Believe me.'

Then he described how the Head had come hurrying out of her room and tripped and fallen across it, and had been sitting on the toilet as the school inspectors drove up outside the front door.

'Oops,' said Mr Walker. 'That's not quite the thing we want to happen on school inspection day, is it?'

'No,' said the jannie, 'And there's another thing you might want to think about. Health and Safety.'

'This toilet,' said Mr Walker loftily, 'is brand new. Untouched by human hand.'

'Or bottom,' someone snickered.

Mr Walker glared at the class. Then he smiled at the jannie. 'I obtained this piece of sanitary ware from my friend who is a builder. I can guarantee that this toilet is unused.'

'It had better stay that way,' the jannie muttered as he stomped off.

***

By the end of morning break the news had spread.

When our class went into the playground the comments were endless. I think I heard every ancient joke about toilets that morning.

The Primary Sevens were the worst. 'We'd rather have no idea for our Enterprise Project than a really crap one like yours!' they yelled at us and then fell about shrieking with laughter.

And it wasn't just jokes – there were riddles and rhymes too.

'Do you know where Mr Walker's class are going on their school trip?'

'Romania?'

'No. *Pooh* Mania.'

'Who wrote the book *I've got to go now?*'

'Lydia Laverty!'

Even the Infants joined in. Two little kids in Primary One ran up to me in the playground.

'Why did Tigger stick his head down the toilet?' one of them called out.

And before I could reply the other shouted back. 'He was looking for Winnie the Pooh!'

Then they giggled hysterically the way Primary Ones do, and ran away.

At lunchtime I thought it safer to eat my packed lunch in the classroom.

Most of my classmates joined me. It was too much to take, being outside and having to listen to the teasing. Then Mr Walker drifted in with his own sandwich box.

'The Head is lunching with the school inspectors in the staffroom,' he said. 'I thought it best to keep a low profile.'

Salikah, who had gone home for lunch, came bursting in. 'Have you heard the latest?' she said. 'The whole school is calling us the WCs.'

'It's a pun,' explained Mr Walker. 'Originally a toilet was known as a Water Closet, hence WC. And the initial letters from the two words, "Walker's Class" also gives the abbreviation WC.'

Everybody looked at me

They never said anything, but I knew what they were thinking. It was all my fault.

Mr Walker must have noticed because he spoke up. 'Don't blame Jamie. Everyone voted for his idea, myself included. So we stick together. One for all, and all for one.'

'Well, if we're keeping the toilet in the classroom a Number One is better than a Number Two,' said Martin.

'Very funny,' I said bitterly.

'Actually,' Mr Walker laughed, 'that *is* quite funny.'

At that moment someone knocked at the classroom door. Heather, who was nearest, opened it up.

There was a Primary Three kid standing there. 'Is it true that you've got a toilet in there?'

'What's it to you?' said Heather.

'Can I see it?'

'It'll cost you 10p,' said Heather.

Heather was joking, but this little guy pulled 10p from his pocket and handed it to her. Heather glanced at Mr Walker. He nodded and said. 'That can be the first contribution to the Charitable Cause.'

Heather took the money and stood aside.

The Primary Three kid walked over and had a good look

Then he went away. A few seconds later we saw him out in the playground waving his arms and pointing to our classroom. The next thing he was back with some of his mates.

'They want to see it too,' he said.

They all had 10ps clutched in their hands. Ben collected the money and led them over to the toilet. They stood round in a circle staring at it for a minute.

'Can I touch it?' one of them asked.

Ben shrugged. 'I don't see why not.'

'But that's an extra 5p,' Heather said quickly.

Right away they all paid an extra 5p.

Mr Walker raised an eyebrow. 'I think we might be on to something here,' he said.

We held a quick conference to decide a few things, like how to collect the money.

Salikah suggested buying a clear toilet lid and asking the jannie to cut a slot in it and make the toilet itself into a bank.

Everybody thought it was a great idea.

'It would be a good gimmick for the younger children,' she said.

Mr Walker grabbed his jacket. 'I've got time to nip out to the retail park before lunch break ends.'

By that afternoon our toilet's see-through lid with slot was firmly attached. Then we made steps leading up to it and covered them in red cloth. Heather and Ben printed off pictures of the African school from the Internet and stuck them onto display boards to show where the money was going.

We held a full Class Council to sort out our business plan. We agreed that the little ones would pay money to look at a toilet but the older ones might not. So we needed something else to encourage the older children to donate to our cause.

I remembered Mr Walker laughing earlier at Martin's joke.

'Maybe we could collect all the jokes and funny remarks and puns,' I said, 'and do something with those.'

We made up joke sheets to sell. Mr Walker insisted on checking them and deleting the very rude ones. He said he was accepting non-flushing jokes only.

We produced fast facts about toilets, with interesting items like all the different names people use for it – the gents, the ladies, the smallest room in the house, the privy, the cludgie, the can, the outhouse, and the rest.

We did lots of research on waste disposal. Did you know you can actually go on a visit to the sewers in Paris?

All this helped us with our environment project. Since I read up on this I'm going to be a lot more careful. Those cotton buds that are so useful for cleaning in between the computer keyboard keys and getting glue on models, well, they're a pollution nightmare.

***

But the best bit was how we got Primary Seven to contribute to our Charitable Cause.

They still hadn't come up with an original idea for their Enterprise Project. The pressure was on them, for the inspectors were due to visit their class during the week. On Tuesday morning we had an approach from their teacher Ms Baxter.

The Primary Sevens had decided that they wanted to make savings banks in the shape of a lavatory pan with a slot in the seat to put the money in and the opening at the bottom. Making and selling these would be their Enterprise Project.

Mr Walker said they'd have to pay us a fee. After all it had all been our idea. 'Especially Jamie's,' he smiled at me.

Ms Baxter went away and members of the Primary Seven Enterprise Committee came to talk to us. They offered us ten pounds.

We had a whole class meeting to discuss their offer.

'Suppose they sell fifty million of them banks?' said Martin.

'*Those* banks,' Mr Walker corrected him. 'What is your point?'

'We need a cut,' said Martin.

'I think you'll find that's a licensing agreement with a profit percentage,' said Mr Walker.

'No, a cut,' said Ben. 'And if they don't pay up then we go along and sort them out.'

'Business doesn't have to be like that,' said Mr Walker hurriedly. 'Negotiation is the way forward.'

'There should be Fair Trade,' agreed Heather.

'Yes,' said Mr Walker. 'They've got to make a profit too. Work it out for yourselves. From their profit comes ours. If we don't let them make money, then they won't make enough to pay us.'

So we charged them, but not too much. For every bank they made they had to give us 20p towards our Toilet Fund. We insisted on inspection rights to make sure they were using recycleable materials, and had good working conditions.

'We have a responsibility to see that they don't exploit their workers,' said Mr Walker.

'The person who's being exploited is me,' moaned their teacher, Ms Baxter. 'I haven't had a tea break since this project began.'

***

The School Inspector's Report came in.

The Head read it out at whole school assembly.

'"Innovative and interesting things are happening in this school,"' she read.

She actually smiled at our class.

We're still known in the school as the WCs.

But we don't care.

Last week we got some photographs and a podcast emailed to us from Africa. It showed all the school children queuing to use their new toilet. They'd made a big sign that read 'Thank you Primary Six'. They were waving their hands and shouting and smiling at us.

Mrs Walker printed one of the photographs and we made them into badges and stickers. It's the new 'must-have' thing to wear.

The Head bought one from us for five pounds.

As a reward Mr Walker treated the whole class to an ice cream and it was such a lovely day that he took us to the local park to eat it. In that part of Africa on a warm day the temperature can go to over 40 degrees. A lot of the children have to walk several miles to reach the school. By the time they arrive they are so hot they can't do their work.

They need a shower cubicle.

Mr Walker says he's going to speak to his builder friend at the weekend.

I only hope the Head Teacher looks where she's going when she walks out of her office on Monday morning.

Funny Money

by Alison Prince

There used to be a dress shop down our road called Mandy's. I bought my red skirt there, and a couple of tops. But after a bit they never had anything new, then there was a sale that seemed to go on forever, and then it closed. Dad said they'd gone bankrupt.

Bankrupt? What did that mean? *Bang – krupt.* I said, 'It sounds like something blew up.'

'That's about right,' Dad said. 'It means you've gone bust. Can't pay your bills, debts all over the place. It happens to a lot of people.'

It sounded scary. I said, 'It won't happen to us, will it?'

Dad laughed and said, 'Not on your life. We're the lucky sort. Touch wood.' And he tapped himself on the head, for wood. It was one of his silly jokes.

***

That was over a year ago. Then things started to change. Dad didn't do jokes any more, he went all bad tempered and worried. And Mum got kind of touchy. I reminded her about my pocket money, and she snapped, 'Shannon, for goodness' sake!' She and Dad started arguing. He said she bought too many clothes, and she said, 'What about all your sports stuff, then?' She had a point. The spare room was absolutely jammed – surf board, exercise bike, golf clubs, skis, fishing gear – not to mention the work-bench and things like electric planers and saws, from when Dad was keen on DIY. But I didn't know things were really wrong until the end of the summer term.

I'd been wondering where we were going on holiday. We usually went to Spain, but my friend Sasha kept telling me about this Greek island they'd been to. She showed me the photos, and it really did look wonderful. So I mentioned Greek islands to Mum and Dad once or twice, but they just said things like, 'We'll see', or 'Don't pester'. But I really wanted to know, so I caught Mum while she was doing the ironing and asked what the plans were.

She frowned a bit, and turned away to hang up the shirt she'd just finished. She hates ironing. Then she said, as if she was talking to the shirt, 'I think we'll just spend some time with Gran.'

I didn't get it. I said, 'But we see Gran lots. And Arbroath's not abroad.' It's just up the coast from Dundee, you can drive there from Glasgow in an hour.

Mum picked up another shirt and said, 'It's seaside.'

'But it isn't hot, and there's no cafes on the pavement,' I argued. 'And it smells of smoked haddock.'

'You like smoked haddock,' Mum said.

'I've gone off it.' I hadn't really, but I was cross.

Mum stood the iron on its end, and sighed. She said, 'The thing is, Shannon, we've got a big problem about money.'

In that moment, it was like everything had turned upside down. I knew now why she and Dad had gone so ratty. We were broke.

I didn't know what to say. I'd never thought of us as rich, but Mum had a wallet with about twenty plastic cards in it – and if you've got cards, you've got money, haven't you? That's the way it always seemed, anyway. Every Saturday, she and I went shopping. It was our favourite thing. 'Shop till we drop,' we used to say, and laugh. So what had gone wrong?

Mum seemed to know what I was thinking. She said, 'Credit cards are so easy. But if you don't pay for what you've spent by the end of the month, the credit card people charge a lot of interest. So you owe them more and more. Then they say you have to pay up, right now.'

'And that's happened to us?'

'Well, yes,' Mum said. 'So we can't manage a holiday this year. But I'll make it up to you, darling, I promise.'

She gave me a brave smile and I tried to smile back, I really did. But what was I going to say to Sasha and the others? They were all going somewhere great, like Greece and France and Canada, and when they heard about Arbroath, they'd give me pitying looks and say things like, 'Oh, you poor thing'. They might not want to know me any more. My family had gone broke, like Mandy's dress shop. We were a failure.

I bolted out of the room and up the stairs. I was in floods of tears by the time I got to the top, and my bedroom door somehow banged shut behind me. Mum would think I'd slammed it, though I didn't mean to, and that made things even worse.

***

A week later, I was in Arbroath, with Gran. She lives in the top-floor flat of a big old house that overlooks the sea. Dad and Mum stayed for the weekend, then they drove back to Glasgow. 'We're very busy at work,' Dad said.

He runs a taxi hire firm. He started with just one cab that he drove himself, but there are 23 of them now, and he stays in the office, taking orders and passing them to Mrs Khan to put out on the cab radios. I always thought he made lots of money.

Mum works for an estate agent, showing people round houses they might want to buy, and she made the same excuse. 'Summer's a busy time.' She bought a new car last year because she said the clients expected a nice experience. It must have been very expensive.

She and Dad didn't say anything about money problems while they were at Gran's – at least, not while I was listening. But on the Sunday morning Gran asked me to get her a paper from the corner shop, and some tomatoes for lunch. When I came back a woman from downstairs was coming out of the front door with her dog, so she let me in and I didn't have to press the buzzer that sounded in Gran's flat. I climbed all the stairs, and when I got to our door I could hear Dad's voice. He sounded really ratty.

'We don't have any choice,' he was saying. 'We can't keep going. You don't live in the real world, Mum, you don't realise how much money it costs to—'

I didn't want to hear any more, so I rang the bell. Everyone put on big smiles when I came in, and Dad took the paper and went into the other room. Mum set the table and Gran and I sliced the tomatoes for a salad to go with – wouldn't you guess? – smoked haddock.

***

Mum gave me some money on the Sunday afternoon. I didn't really want to take it, but she closed my fingers round the little roll of notes and said, 'Go on. It's the least I can do.'

Dad was outside, putting stuff in the car.

I said, 'Mum, you don't have to. I've been saving up my pocket money, I'm all right.' I had nearly seven pounds.

'I feel so bad about your holiday,' Mum said. 'At least you can buy yourself something nice. And don't worry – it's just funny money.' That's what she called it when we went shopping. Funny money. Money for fun.

I counted the notes after she and Dad had gone. She'd given me £50.

***

A day or two later, Gran and I got the bus into Dundee for a shopping trip. Gran's not like Mum, though. She isn't really into shopping. She didn't pick anything up and hold it against herself to see if it suited her. She just kind of gazed round as if the big store was a nice view.

I asked her, 'Isn't there anything you want?'

'Not really, darling,' Gran said.

'But you might find something fabulous,' I told her. 'Something you never knew you wanted.'

She smiled at me and said, 'I remember feeling like that. Such a thrill, isn't it, taking a new thing home.' Then she went on, 'But new things don't stay new for long, do they? After a few days, they're part of all your other stuff. So you have to go shopping again.'

'It's not you have to,' I said. 'You just want to. Because it's fun.'

Gran said, 'It can get to be a habit, though. If you don't shop, you feel as if you're missing something.'

'But you *might* be missing something,' I said. 'The perfect thing could be sitting there, just waiting for you to find it.'

'Ah,' said Gran, 'now, that's true. The perfect thing is out there somewhere. But you don't always find it through shopping.'

I was going to ask what she meant, but she suggested a cup of tea, so we went and found a cafe. I had a mango and banana smoothie. I wanted to pay for it, but Gran said it was her treat.

I asked, 'Can we do some more shopping?' I thought Gran might be fed up with it, but she said, 'Of course we can.'

I started turning over the price tags on things to see what they cost. Most of the clothes seemed very expensive. When Mum and I went shopping, I never even knew what we'd spent. Like she said, it was all so easy.

I stopped to look at a short dress that you could wear over trousers or on its own. It had pink sequins all round the neck and I loved it, but it was £65. Even with my saved-up pocket money added to Mum's £50, I didn't have enough.

I came back from that shopping trip with nothing new at all except a pen with a green feather on the end and a postcard of boats in Dundee in the old days, to send to Mum. And those came out of my pocket money.

I had a weird dream that night. Mum and Dad and I were living in a tree, in a kind of basket. I suppose it was a nest really, but it didn't seem like that. Bits of the basket kept unravelling, so there were gaps and holes, and I was clutching Mum tight because I thought we were going to fall out.

***

At breakfast, I said, 'Gran, have you ever been broke?'

I felt my face turn red because it was kind of about Mum and Dad, and they might not want me to talk about it, but Gran didn't seem bothered. In fact, she laughed.

'Oh, yes,' she said. 'I was never any good at earning money. I stayed at home with my children while they were small, then I did part-time teaching, but you couldn't call it a career. Your grandpa wrote music. People still play his things, but it never made him rich.'

'But how did you manage?' I asked. 'It must have been awful.'

'No,' said Gran. 'It was difficult sometimes, but it wasn't awful. Your grandpa was so taken up with his music, his days were always interesting. And because I was at home with the children, there were lots of things I could do that cut down on how much money we needed.'

'What sort of things?'

'I grew lots of our food – I've always liked gardening. And I never bought ready-made meals and frozen stuff – that's the most expensive way to live. If you've time to cook, you can make soups and stews and pasta dishes that don't cost you much at all. Anyway,' Gran went on, 'what shall we do today? Would you like to go down on the beach?'

'Don't mind,' I said, though I wasn't really very keen. I couldn't see Gran making sandcastles or playing Frisbee.

'You ride a bike, don't you?' she asked.

'Yes – but it's at home.'

'Mine's in the shed downstairs,' Gran said, 'and we'll hire one for you. It doesn't cost much. Then we can go and explore.'

She must be quite old, but she's amazingly fit. We headed off up the coast on our bikes, soon turning off the main road, and came to a place where houses stood high on a cliff. The beach was a mixture of sand and rock.

'It's good here,' Gran said. 'There are caves in the cliff, so you can shelter if it rains. Let's go and find some rock pools.'

That day changed everything.

The pools were very deep, and if you knelt down and looked in, it was like a different world. Little, dark-red sea anemones grew on the sides of the rocks, putting out their fringes of tentacles in

hopes of catching something. If you touched them with a bit of weed, they folded themselves in quickly. I saw one catch a small, transparent shrimp, and it was awful in a way, seeing the shrimp being swallowed up, but at the same time, it was great for the anemone. Little crabs rushed around sideways on the sandy bottom of the pools, and some of them were hermit crabs, living in small winkle shells.

'Tell you what,' Gran said, 'we could set up an aquarium at home if you like. A mini sea-world.'

So we went back the next day with plastic containers and a net – Gran's got a basket on the front of her bike and pannier bags, she can carry lots. When she talked about an aquarium I thought she meant a proper fish tank, with a thing that makes air bubbles and all that, but she gave me a big old preserving pan that she used for making jam. We were very careful about getting some sea snails to keep things clean, and weed that was rooted on stones and a slab of rock with anemones, and I caught lots of shrimps and crabs and a couple of little fish.

'We'll need to give them some fresh sea water quite often,' Gran said, so we had an expedition to the beach every day, and came back with plastic bottles of water and sometimes some new creatures to add to our sea-world. We went into the caves, too, and there were gulls nesting on high ledges in some of them. And we found a place where a sea otter

lived. He was a very untidy eater – there were fish bones all over the place. I wished I could see him, but he didn't appear.

On the last day before I had to go home, we took all the creatures from my aquarium back to the beach in plastic containers of water, and returned them carefully to their rock pool.

That evening I said, 'I wish I could be by the sea all the time. There must be lots more things to find.'

'M'm,' said Gran thoughtfully. 'When you grow up, you could be a marine biologist. That's someone who studies the sea and all the things that live in it. You'd learn deep-sea diving, too. That would be really exciting.'

'Wow! Do you think I could?'

'Why not?' said Gran. 'This is the right time to start. Get stuck into your work at school, make sure you do biology, go to university and there you are. Dabbling about in the sea for a living.'

It was a weird idea. I'd never thought school had anything to do with whatever wild dreams I might have. The thing I'd always looked forward to was being out of school and spending money – but everything was different now. I stared at Gran and ideas were racing about in my head. Some of them were a bit scary.

'Won't it be too hard?' I asked. 'I might not be clever enough.'

'Of course you are,' Gran said. 'It's only work. And work is the best thing in the world if you enjoy it.'

***

Just after I got home, a lady with a briefcase came, and there was a long talk between her and Mum and Dad. I was in the kitchen, reading a book about sea life that I got from the library, so I didn't hear what went on, but after she'd gone, Mum said things were looking better.

I asked, 'What about the credit card people?'

'We've made arrangements,' she said. 'We'll pay them a certain amount every month. We're going to get things really organised.'

Dad was looking relieved. He said, 'At least we can keep the house.'

And that scared me – I didn't know we might have ended up with nowhere to live.

The next day, we piled all the sports stuff and racks of clothes into the garage, so the spare room was empty. 'We'll do it up and let it to a student,' Mum said.

We had Car Boot Sales every Saturday for weeks. Dad kept the bench and most of the tools, though. He says it's cheaper to do your own household repairs and decoration – he'd just got into the habit of paying someone else because it was easier.

We've still got Mum's car, but Dad sold his. We live quite near his taxi office, so he's going to bike down there every day. He patted his tummy and said, 'Lose a bit of weight, too. Can't be bad.' We'd sold the exercise bike – Dad said it seemed daft to ride a pretend bike in a bedroom when you could ride a real one to work.

I put a notice in the pet shop, saying I'd take dogs for walks. I do two Labradors after school every day and a poodle on Saturday mornings. I'm saving the money to buy a fish tank.

I gave the £50 back to Mum. She didn't want to take it, but I closed her fingers round the roll of notes like she did when she gave it to me, and said, 'Go on. I don't need it.'

She looked as if she was going to cry, but I said, 'Mum, don't worry about it. Like you said, it was just funny money.'

I'm not sure if money is ever really funny, but it made Mum laugh. So that was OK.

Charlie Fly and the Nice Dream

by Nicola Morgan

Business was dead at Charlie Fly (Private Eye). The summer holidays were already three days old and we'd had zero customers. Not even one lost key or cat.

Charlie was examining his toenails through my magnifying glass. Charlie is brainy but I didn't see how even *he* could find answers in his toenails.

I was looking at my computer screen. 'Jobs,' it said. The rest of the screen was empty. I scrolled to the next page. 'Money,' it said. That page was empty too.

Charlie is the clever one; but I'm the one with the computer so I am important. Charlie has to share his with his sisters, which is a nightmare for anyone trying to run a business. Can you imagine Richard Branson sharing a computer with his sisters? No, exactly. Mind you, can you imagine him examining his toenails with a magnifying glass?

My name is Fly and Charlie's name is Charlie. I'm called Fly because I can run very fast. This could be useful because we are private detectives, but it has not been useful yet. Except when old Mr Lambert chased us for spying on him, but I'd rather forget that.

We can investigate any problem you might have. Like, is that really the gas man or is he an international spy? Or, if you have lost your hamster or your cat or your key, we could definitely find it for you. Well, not definitely, but maybe. And if fast running is necessary, you've come to the right place.

But if you have anything more exciting than that, please tell us. Hamsters and cats and keys are very important but we'd be even more interested in cracking an international spy ring. We keep our eyes open for things like that. Once, we followed a man from the High Street to Bothwell Road (which is a long way, in case you don't know it) because some suspicious white powder was coming out of his carrier bag. It could have been drugs or poison, so we didn't get too close. But it was a bag of flour. We discovered this when we crept up to his window and heard his wife using extremely bad language.

We have everything detectives need. Walkie talkies, notebooks, magnifying glasses and finger-print powder. Well, flour. Charlie has a camera. And we have cards saying Charlie Fly (Private Eye), which I did on my computer.

It's extremely exciting being private detectives. Or it would be if we had any customers. Then we could earn some money. But we are not in it for the money. We have something my dad calls 'job satisfaction'. He says sometimes you can have money and sometimes you can have job satisfaction.

Personally, I'd like both. I would get a lot of satisfaction out of having loads of money.

Charlie had finished exploring his toenails and I was about to play a computer game. It's amazing how much inspiration a computer game can bring. No, it's not really amazing but I couldn't think what else to do. If customers won't come, I can't force them.

Just then the phone rang downstairs but I ignored it. I have parents to answer the phone. It's better than a secretary because you don't have to pay parents.

The computer game was nearly ready to start. Then my secretary called up the stairs, 'Fly, here please! Hurry!'

OK, not my secretary – Mum. Charlie and I went downstairs, where Mum was flapping. She likes flapping at home because she can't flap at work. She's a librarian and libraries are peaceful places where flapping is not allowed.

'Panic stations, Fly! Olivia's coming. I'm collecting her from the airport this afternoon.'

'Who's Olivia?'

'Your cousin, for goodness' sake.'

'Oh, Olive Oil.'

'And you'd better stop calling her that. You're going to have to get on with her. She's coming for six weeks.'

'Aghh! Why?'

'Uncle Joe's broken his leg.'

'What about Aunt Sarah?' I wailed.

'She's filming. In Mongolia.'

'Can't she come back? They're rich enough, aren't they? They don't need the money she earns – you said so.'

'No, I didn't. Of course I didn't. When did I? Anyway, she'd be letting a lot of people down. It'll be nice, Fly. You and Charlie don't have anything to do this summer…'

'We have a business to run,' I pointed out.

'Olivia can help you,' said Mum. 'She's probably good at things like that, what with her dad being so ri… um… ridiculously clever at business. She could be your finance director.'

'She could be my secretary, more like,' I muttered.

'We'd have to share our profits with her, wouldn't we?' asked Charlie.

'Do you *have* any profits?' asked Mum.

'Not as such,' he replied. 'Just job satisfaction.'

'Well, just think, you could have a lot more job satisfaction if you had some profits. Now stop whingeing and go and vacuum the house while I make a shopping list.' And she went off, muttering about strawberries and expensive ice cream and the sort of posh food I only get if I've done something special or I'm ill. When I don't feel like food at all.

I've read books where authors talk about sinking feelings and heavy hearts. Well, I know what they mean. In a book, at this point the sun would go behind a cloud. I looked out of the window. Sure enough, massive grey clouds everywhere.

***

Normally I see Olive Oil once a year. They are stinking rich and Mum says it's awkward. I don't think it's awkward, just unfair. They moved south when Olive Oil was a baby. Anyway, now we usually just see them near Christmas. But last Christmas Olive Oil's family went to South Africa to buy a holiday house. Uncle Joe owns a company that makes lots of money and Aunt Sarah makes films that make lots of money. I expect they also have job satisfaction.

But you can't have everything. Great profits, great job satisfaction, creepy daughter.

So, that's why I had a heavy heart and a Titanic-sized sinking feeling as we waited for her to arrive.

There was our car. And there was Olive Oil. She'd changed in the eighteen months since I'd seen her. I'd remembered her with silly pigtails and pink fairy bobbles, and clothes that seemed to matter if they got a speck of dirt on them. But now her hair was big and shiny and long, and she wore jeans with scruffy edges and quite normal-looking trainers. She was taller than me and Charlie, even though she was the same age.

Why are girls so confident? She gave Dad a kiss and said how kind it was of us to have her. She smiled at me and Charlie and said hello. Luckily, she didn't kiss me.

I didn't know what to say while we were all showing her where everything was. Dad made a rude comment about how my bedroom smelt, and said something about how we were detectives but it would be surprising if we could detect the carpet there was so much stuff on it.

'Let's leave them to play,' said Mum, and off they went. *Play?* Why do parents always think kids play? We have a business to run and no time to be entertaining rich cousins.

Olivia saw my computer was on. 'Cool,' she said. 'You've got Shock Tactix! Can I have a go?'

Half an hour and two computer games later, I realised the summer might not be totally ruined after all. Although she had a posh voice and you could *tell* she was rich, she was not that bad. She was even *quite* good at my computer game.

The next day, I decided she was definitely OK, because she told me I was brilliant when I accidentally came up with an idea that would save our business.

Every business needs a person with ideas and I have decided that's me.

What happened was this. We were having a meeting. By the way, I'd invited Olive Oil to join our business. This was partly because Mum had dropped me in it by saying, 'Olivia can help you with your business, can't she, Fly?' And Olive Oil had looked all smiley and *interested*. And partly because she had money and we might need some. All businesses need money to get them going. It has a special name but I've forgotten it.

So, the meeting. We were lying on Portobello beach, just down the road from our house. Charlie was scanning the horizon with binoculars and making notes in his notebook. Olive Oil was playing a game on her phone.

I was thinking. I was thinking that being a private eye was not a good way to make money. And there wasn't even much job satisfaction right then.

'Here's what I think,' I said, in a business-y voice. 'We need to earn some money.'

'Good idea,' said Olive Oil.

'But you could just ask your parents for money,' said Charlie to her.

'They don't believe in giving me lots of money,' she said.

'But that's mean,' said Charlie. 'They're loaded.'

'They don't want me to be spoilt.'

'So how come you've got money in your purse?' I asked. Well, I couldn't help peering over her shoulder, could I?

'I've got birthday money saved up, and my dad gave me some for emergencies while I'm staying with you.'

Fair enough. Olive Oil was really not that different from us. I think I might stop calling her Olive Oil.

'So, how did your dad make lots of money?' I asked.

'He says all businesses need the same thing. It's the secret of success. He wrote a book about it.'

Crikey. He writes books too. He MUST be loaded. Maybe he knows J.K. Rowling.

Charlie looked at me. I looked at Charlie. 'Well?' we asked.

'He says the secret of success is to find something people want and then sell it to them at the highest price they will pay.'

We were silent. The sun beat down. I was sweating. It wasn't a very helpful secret.

We were silent some more. I had no ideas. None at all.

'I'm thirsty,' I said. 'Let's get an ice cream.'

The shop was on the way home. A boy who lives near me was working there. He's in senior school. Liam, he's called. He's got sweaty skin and an earring. And scary hair that's so short it's almost invisible.

'Haven't you got anything cheaper?' asked Olivia, rummaging in the freezer. 'And sort of plainer?'

He was staring at Olivia as though he really fancied her. *Eughhh.* Him, I mean, not her.

'What about your boyfriends?' he said. 'They're cheaper. And plainer.'

Olivia stared at him for a moment. 'We'll go somewhere else. We wouldn't buy anything from you if you paid us,' she said coolly. And we walked out.

'Aye, suit yourself. I'll be here if you change your mind,' he called after us in a leery sort of voice.

'So, where else is there?' asked Olivia, scowling.

'Nowhere,' said Charlie. 'You've just lost us our only chance of ice cream before we get home.'

He was right. And I was very hot and thirsty. I watched some kids walk into the shop and come out with expensive ice creams. Must have cost a fortune.

That was when I had my idea. I knew I was the ideas person.

And that was how we came to be making ice cream later that afternoon in our kitchen. Olivia had used her money to buy lemons, sugar and cream, and I'd persuaded the greengrocer to sell us over-ripe bananas extra cheap. Then we bought a pack of 200 plastic cups and a pack of 200 plastic spoons. Olivia seemed to know what we needed.

Charlie wrote down the costs in his notebook.

At my house, we started to make lemon ices and banana creams.

It wasn't as easy as we'd thought. In fact, being a private eye was a lot easier. Probably because we had no customers. Life is easy if you have no customers. But there's no money and no job satisfaction.

If you'd seen the kitchen you'd have thought we were completely out of control. OK, we *were* completely out of control. Every bowl was out and every surface was covered. The floor was sticky with lemon and slimy with banana and crunchy with sugar. The dog thought she was in heaven.

All we needed was for my mum to come in. My mum came in.

I won't go into what she said and the look on her face and the fact that she had to sit down very suddenly. On something slimy. But once we'd explained, she calmed down. A bit.

'You need a division of labour,' she said.

I looked at Charlie and Charlie looked at me. What?

Olivia nodded. 'You mean one of us should do this and the others should do something else.'

'What else?' asked Charlie.

'Well,' said Mum, 'you'll need to advertise, and make posters, and think of a name, and decide prices, and where to sell the things, and find a table, and plenty of change, and a coolbox to keep them frozen while you sell them, and make space in the garage freezer and…'

I was glad to get out of that kitchen. To be honest, I was feeling sick. But we had to taste the products *very* often, otherwise how could we know our customers would like them?

Charlie picked up his notebook and licked banana cream off it. 'You have ideas and I'll write them down,' he said.

'And afterwards you'll all clean the kitchen,' said Mum.

'We could pay you to do it,' I said.

'I am much too expensive,' said Mum.

***

We called our new business Nice Dream. That was my idea as well.

The first day of Nice Dream was amazing. People had to pass our house on their way to the beach, and our ices were cheaper than shop ices. And we gave a few free samples and told everyone to tell their friends.

So, by the time Liam came past at four o'clock, we had nearly sold our first batch. He was walking back from his job, looking tired and sweatier than ever.

'Lemon Nice, Liam?' I called. 'Only a few left!'

'Banana Dream, Liam?' called Charlie, grinning. 'Get 'em while they're cold!'

Liam slouched over. 'You allowed to do this?' he asked, sneering.

'Why not?' asked Olivia. 'People want to buy them. It's a free country.'

'Is it?' drawled Liam. He paused. 'You been cleared by Health and Safety?'

Sinking feeling. Big time. Horror washed over me like some cold wave full of bits of slimy seaweed and dead fish. Liam's dad works for a thing called Health and Safety. He inspects restaurants. He makes rules about things like washing hands and checking that fridges are cold.

Mind you, you have to feel a bit sorry for Liam's dad. I mean, there can't be much job satisfaction OR money in inspecting people's hands and fridges.

But, there was definitely something menacing in Liam's face. And when he picked up one of our ices, coughed on it and then put it back, there was something even worse than menacing.

Then he and his friends started kicking a ball nearby, and spitting, and with bits of mud flying around and boys shouting, no more customers came near. He knocked over a pile of Charlie Fly cards that we had on the stall, and laughed as he picked one up and read it:

Charlie Fly
(Private Eye)

Lost it? We can find it.

Puzzled? We can solve it.

If we don't, you don't pay!

He put it in his pocket, pretending to be an interested customer, and I didn't like the thought of it being there.

Still, we'd almost sold our first batch – nearly 50 ices altogether. And we weren't going to leave while Liam was there, so we stuck it out, and then we cleared up, leaving no rubbish. Of course, we weren't going to leave any rubbish anyway but Dad came home just then, bought the last Banana Dream, and said something about how businesses must respect the environment. He even picked some things up for us, including jumpers and shoes and sunglasses and things that we'd left lying around when we got too hot. We stuffed everything in bags.

Then, of course, we had to get busy making more ice creams for tomorrow.

'Make sure you wash your hands,' I said to Olivia, who glared at me.

'Why is Olivia doing the kitchen stuff?' asked Dad. 'Isn't that sex discrimination?'

Charlie looked at me and I looked at Charlie. Was it? But it wasn't that Olivia was a girl, was it? She was just better at making ices.

'Have you seen the boys' hands?' asked Mum. 'Think about health and safety.'

I shuddered. Liam's dad. Inspecting our hands and our fridge.

Charlie had been adding up some figures in his notebook. 'Hey!' he said. 'Guess what?'

I looked at Olivia and Olivia looked at me. 'What?'

'We made a profit!' We all looked at each other. 'Even after we've paid back Olivia's investment.' That was the word.

'Wow!' I said.

'And we have the assets, of course,' said Olivia.

'What?' I said.

'Assets, stupid,' said Charlie.

'Oh, right. I thought you said asses.' Charlie looked at Olivia and Olivia looked at Charlie.

Later that evening, when Olivia was in another room, I asked Mum what our assets were. 'The things you bought which you've still got. Like the extra plastic cups and spoons. So if you sell all your ices tomorrow as well, you'll make even more profit because you won't have to buy more things. And you've still got plenty of ingredients left too.'

Wow. So we'd made a profit. One day we'd be rich.

***

Unfortunately not. Next day it rained. And the next day too. We stared at the grey skies. Our ices stayed in the freezer.

Nice Dream was nothing more than a nice dream.

Except for one thing. Olivia had an idea. It was, I admit, a good idea, and it might have worked. Except that we never got as far as trying because something happened.

Olivia's idea was to make hot lemon drinks instead of ice creams, and sell them to wet shoppers. She said businesses must 'adapt to new circumstances'. Mum said, 'Yes, and diversify, too.' Olivia nodded wisely, but I don't think even *she* had a clue what Mum meant. Nor did I.

More importantly, we checked with Mum whether this would work, health and safety-wise. She said it would if we heated them properly. 'That'll be 50p for professional consultancy,' she said.

'Get real, Mum,' I said.

'To be honest,' said Charlie, 'there was no contract, so we are not obliged to pay you a penny.' Sometimes, you can tell Charlie's mum works at Citizen's Advice.

'You can tell your mum works at Citizen's Advice,' said Mum.

So, we got out the bags of stuff that we'd brought in from the garden on the day we sold our ices. We would need to change the posters and prices and everything. A lot of thinking must be done to get this new business going. Diversifying was hard work, whatever it was. Olivia went on about how it was good to manage risk. I just thought it seemed like common sense. I didn't see that it needed special words, but Charlie and Olivia can't do things without using big words.

'We should have a meeting,' I said.

'We are having a meeting,' said Olivia.

'But Charlie isn't taking notes. It can't be a meeting if someone isn't taking notes.'

'Minutes,' said Charlie. Whatever.

Charlie got out his notebook and I was about to say something important when the doorbell rang. My secretary-mother had gone out so we all went to answer it.

It was Liam. Looking odd. Not horrible and fierce. Well, actually, he was looking horrible but it was a different sort of horrible. Horrible and worried. And he was holding a scrumpled Charlie Fly (Private Eye) card.

'Can you really do this?' he asked. 'Like find something that's lost?'

'Of course,' said Charlie confidently. 'It's what detectives do. It's the whole point.'

'Why?' asked Olivia. 'Have you lost something?'

'My phone,' he said. 'And my dad's mad at me.'

'Are you taking notes?' I asked Charlie. Charlie was. 'So,' I said to Liam, 'are you asking us to find your phone?'

'As in *commissioning* us, Liam?' added Olivia.

'Yeah, but what's it cost if you find it?' he asked.

'£19.99,' I said firmly. 'Plus expenses.'

'How quickly can you find it?' he asked. He was looking really worried. I almost felt sorry for him. Almost.

'It's a tricky one,' said Charlie. 'We can only do our best.'

'I'll pay you an extra fiver if you find it today.'

'We can't promise anything,' said Olivia.

Then Charlie took more notes while we asked questions. Things like, what the phone looked like and all the places he had been on the day he lost it. We even asked him all the places he'd been to the toilet in that same day, which was extremely amusing. He had been to the toilet in some seriously weird places.

'Don't call us, we'll call you,' I said.

'He can't call us – he hasn't got his phone,' said Charlie.

'Oh, of course,' I smiled. 'You haven't got your phone, have you? But we'll call your home when we find it.'

'Don't tell my mum or dad,' pleaded Liam.

'Don't worry, we won't tell your mum or dad. Or your gran. Or your sisters. Or your dog. Or anyone else at all.'

He left and we did high fives all round. 'Charlie Fly (Private Eye), we're back in business!' Charlie shouted.

'The sun's come out,' noticed Olivia. 'We can sell ice creams again. While we think how to find his phone.'

So we started to get everything out of the bags, the bags which we hadn't emptied since the day when we sold all those ices… And that was when I found it. The phone. In one of the bags.

It must have fallen out of his pocket when he was messing around. Served him right.

'Wow!' said Charlie. 'THAT was easy money!'

'Yes, and that's what Liam will say too. He might be suspicious. We won't tell him yet,' said Olivia.

'But he said we could have an extra fiver if we find it today,' Charlie pointed out. 'It would be bad business to miss out on extra profit.'

I did some thinking. After all, I am the ideas person. 'If we tell him in a couple of hours and also NOT take his extra fiver, he will be so pleased that he might use us again and tell his friends,' I said.

'Brilliant idea, Fly!' said Olivia. Charlie nodded carefully. I could tell he was worried about missing that extra profit but, the way I saw it, we'd make more profit if Liam told everyone how clever we were.

A couple of hours later, Liam came round in answer to our phone call. 'How did you find it?' he asked, actually smiling, and Liam smiling was even more horrible than Liam looking normal.

'We can't reveal our methods,' said Charlie.

'It's a trade secret,' explained Olivia.

'That's for us to know and you to wonder about,' I added.

'Well, thanks anyway,' and he paid us. 'I'll tell all my friends about Charlie Fly (Private Eye),' he added, as he left.

'Oh, one thing,' Olivia called after him. 'Do ask Health and Safety to inspect us. At any time.' And we all held out our hands.

'Fridge, Liam?' I asked, pointing towards the kitchen. But he was too busy grinning and texting someone on his mobile phone.

As we celebrated with a free Lemon Nice and Banana Dream each, we realised that we had the best of both worlds: job satisfaction *and* money.

The summer was looking good. We had two businesses to run now. There's probably a name for having several businesses. Millionaire will do me. Maybe, one day, if we work really hard. And if I keep coming up with good ideas. And if Charlie uses his brains.

And Olivia? Well, she's our finance director. And chief cook.

One day, we might even be able to afford to pay Mum to wash up for us. It's a Nice Dream.

No Change

by Jonathan Meres

When Callum and Rory's grandma came for tea, she said what she always said.

'Look at those two. Like peas in a pod.'

Callum smiled.

'If I had a pound for every time you said that, Gran!'

Rory looked at his brother, expecting him to carry on. But he didn't.

'Well?' said Rory.

'Well what?' said Callum.

'How much would you have then? If you had a pound for every time Gran said that?'

'Erm… let me see.'

Callum screwed up his face in concentration.

'£47,' he said at last.

'You're weird,' laughed Rory.

'What's so weird about that?' said Callum. 'Mum! Rory says I'm weird!'

'Now, now you two,' said Mum. 'Wash your hands and get up to the table.'

Callum did as he was told immediately. Rory had to be told another three times.

They were the same but different, Callum and Rory. It was no surprise that they *looked* the same. They *were* twins after all. You'd expect them to look the same. And they did, pretty much. They both had blond hair and blue eyes for a start. They were both tall and skinny. They both had noses that turned up ever so slightly at the end, like miniature ski jumps. If you'd never met them before, it was almost impossible to tell them apart. But they weren't identical. Not *quite* anyway.

Their mum and dad could tell them apart. Their friends could tell them apart too. So could their teachers. But you had to know what to look for. You had to know that Callum was the one with the tiny mole on his chin and that Rory was the one with the slightly chipped front tooth. If you knew that, then you were fine. If you didn't, you'd either have to guess, or ask.

'Which one are you then?'

If Callum was the one who was asked, he'd usually give the right answer. It was less bother that way. It seemed only polite.

'I'm Callum,' Callum would say.

But if Rory was the one who was asked, he'd usually give the *wrong* answer. On purpose. It was more fun that way.

'I'm Callum,' Rory would say, grinning mischievously.

You see, just because they *looked* the same didn't mean they *were* the same. Which is why Callum and Rory were the same but different.

Callum was the calmer of the two. He was more shy and a bit more serious than his brother. He was thought of as 'The Quiet One' – the one most likely to be found with his nose in a book, or playing on the computer. He was also the elder of the twins. Only by ten minutes. But he was the elder nevertheless and Rory had never quite forgiven him.

Rory was forever on the go. Always doing something different, or trying something new. Constantly flitting from one obsession to another and from one hobby to the next, Rory had the concentration span of an ironing board.

When Callum and Rory's grandma was getting ready to leave, she did what she always did. She gave each of her grandsons a pound coin.

'Thanks, Gran,' said Callum.

But Rory said nothing. He was already thinking what he was going to buy with the money.

'Rory?' said Mum. 'What do you say?'

'What?' said Rory. 'Oh right. Sorry, yeah, thanks Gran, that's wicked!'

Gran smiled.

'Don't spend it all at once now, boys,' she said.

'Course not, Gran,' said Callum.

But Rory said nothing.

'Rory?' said Mum. 'Your grandma's talking to you.'

'Sorry, Gran, what was that?' said Rory.

'I said don't spend it all at once,' said Gran.

'OK, Gran,' grinned Rory.

The twins' mum looked at Rory. She knew that if he *didn't* spend it all at once it would be an absolute miracle.

***

'Coming out for a bike ride, Cal?' said Rory.

It wasn't even five minutes since Gran had left. Rory had been fidgeting about like he'd got ants in his pants ever since.

'Er, yeah, all right then,' said Callum.

'Be back soon, Mum, OK?' said Rory, heading for the door.

'Bye, Mum,' said Callum, following on behind. 'Where are we going, Ror?'

But Rory didn't reply. He'd already gone.

'Bye, boys. Take care,' called Mum. *She* knew *exactly* where they were going. They were going to spend the money they'd just been given. Or rather, *Rory* was going to spend the money he'd just been given. Callum was going with him.

As it turned out, Mum was right.

'Why have we stopped?' said Callum approximately two minutes later.

They'd only got as far as the end of the road. Rory had got off his bike and was leaning it against the newsagent's window.

'I thought we were going for a bike ride.'

'Correction,' said Rory. 'We've *been* for a bike ride. You got that pound?'

'Eh?'

'That pound that Gran gave you. You still got it?'

Callum looked at his brother like he'd gone completely mad.

'Course I've still got it!'

'Lend us it then,' said Rory.

'Eh?' said Callum. 'What for?'

'So I can get some football stickers.'

'No way!' said Callum. 'Spend your own money!'

'I haven't got enough.'

'Why? How much are they?'

'35 pence a packet,' said Rory.

Callum did a quick mental calculation.

'So that means you can get two packets then,' he said. 'Two packets would be 70 pence and you'd get 30 pence change.'

'Yeah, but I want more than that, don't I?' said Rory. 'If you lend me *your* pound I could get… er… I could get…'

'Five packets,' said Callum. 'Five packets would cost £1.75.'

'There you go!' said Rory. 'You'd get 25 pence change!'

'No, I wouldn't,' said Callum.

'What do you mean, no, you wouldn't? Yes, you would!' said Rory.

'No, I wouldn't. Because I'm not going to lend it to you in the first place!'

Rory looked like he'd just been told the world was about to end.

'What?'

'I'm saving it.'

'Saving it? But why? You've got loads of money already!'

'That's because I save it!' said Callum.

'But you never *spend* any of it! What's the point of having money if you don't spend it?'

'I'm *going* to spend it,' said Callum. 'Once I've got enough.'

'Enough for what?' said Rory.

'A skateboard.'

'A skateboard?' said Rory. 'Whoa! They're dead expensive!'

'Yeah, I know,' said Callum, rolling his eyes. '*That's* why I'm saving up!'

Rory looked puzzled. He just didn't get this *saving up* thing at all. But then that was another crucial difference between him and his twin brother. Callum always seemed to have money. Rory never had any. Well, at least not for very long anyway.

They were both *given* the same amount of money. £2.50 a week pocket money plus a pound whenever Gran came. But whereas Callum *saved* his, Rory spent his money as soon as possible. He couldn't *help* spending it. It was as if the money was burning a hole in his pocket. He just *had* to spend it before his trousers caught fire! Even if it was on something he didn't particularly want. The possibility of saving the money just didn't enter Rory's head. He couldn't save money if his life depended on it.

'So that's a no then?' said Rory.

'Yes, it's a no,' said Callum.

But Rory was nothing if not determined. He decided to give it one last shot.

'I'll buy you some sweets with the change?'

Callum couldn't quite believe what he was hearing.

'Correction,' he said. '*My* change.'

Honestly, thought Callum. *What was his brother like?*

***

'Can I have some new trainers, please, Mum?' said Rory.

They'd only just got in the door. Callum had eventually agreed to *lend* his brother five pence so that he had £1.05p altogether – enough to buy three packets of football stickers at 35 pence a packet. It was the only way to keep him quiet. Rory was delighted. Not as delighted as he would have been with *five* packets mind! But Callum figured it would keep him happy until the *next* time he wanted to buy something. Which wasn't very long as it turned out. Even by Rory's standards.

'New trainers?' said Mum.

'Yeah. They're silver with these two blue stripes down the side and these wicked yellow laces! I've seen them in this catalogue! They're dead cool! And they're only, like, seventy quid or something!'

Callum and his mum exchanged knowing glances. Rory really didn't have a clue when it came to money. He had no concept of the *value* of money. £70 for trainers, or 35 *pence* for football stickers. It was all the same to Rory. He really *did* appear to think that money grew on trees!

'Did you say *only* seventy quid?' said Mum.

'Yeah, I know. Bargain eh?'

'So that would be £140 on trainers! Just like that!'

Rory groaned. He'd forgotten that Callum would have to have new trainers too.

'Mum you don't *always* have to dress us the same, you know,' said Rory. 'Just because we're twins.'

'It makes life easier,' said Mum.

'For *you*, maybe,' said Rory. 'Not for us. It's getting embarrassing. It's not like we're three or something anymore. We're nearly eleven!'

'I don't mind,' said Callum. 'I quite like dressing the same.'

'Shut up, Cal!' hissed Rory.

'Would *you* like some new trainers, Callum?' asked Mum.

Rory looked at his brother, willing him to say yes. They said that some twins were telepathic and could read each others' minds. Well, now was the chance to find out if Callum could read *his*!

'Erm… not really,' said Callum. 'The ones I've got are fine, thanks, Mum.'

Rory could have sworn. So much for telepathic twins!

'There's your answer then I'm afraid, Rory,' said Mum.

'What? So I can't have them then?' said Rory. 'All because of goody two trainers here?'

'Sorry, love, but you don't actually *need* them. You *want* them,' said Mum.

Mum smiled, sympathetically. But Rory was having none of it. His mum was wrong. He *did* need those trainers! He *needed* them like he'd never needed anything before. He was fed up with people saying no to him. Why couldn't they just say yes instead? Was that really too much to ask?

'If you *needed* them that would be different,' said Mum.

Rory thought about that for a moment.

'Really?' he said.

'Of course!' laughed Mum. 'We couldn't have you running round in trainers with holes in, could we?'

Hmm, thought Rory to himself. *Interesting. Very interesting.*

'Well?' said Mum. 'Could we?'

'What?' said Rory. 'Er, no, Mum. Don't suppose we could.'

Callum glanced across at his brother. He recognised that look in Rory's eyes. He knew he was up to something. But what?

***

'You asleep yet, Cal?' whispered Rory.

'No, why?' replied Callum.

'Nothing. Just wondered.'

'I'll let you know when I am if you like.'

'Shut up.'

The twins were lying in bed. Callum, being the elder by ten minutes, was in the top bunk. Rory was in the bottom bunk. It was way after ten o'clock. *Match of the Day* was blasting out of the TV in the front room. It was so loud it was like being at the match itself, except of course that at the match you didn't get a commentator shrieking hysterically in your ear every couple of seconds.

'Rooney chests the ball down! He turns! Shoots! One-nil!'

Rory waited and waited. *He* was wide awake. Not because of the volume of the TV, but because he had a plan. And in order for the plan to work, he needed his brother to be asleep.

Eventually, Rory became aware that Callum had stopped moving around in the bunk above. His breathing had become heavier. He was pretty sure that he'd dropped off. It was time for action.

He got out of bed as quietly as possible and crept along the corridor. He could hear his mum splashing about in the bath and singing to herself. Rory knew she'd be there for ages. He tiptoed downstairs and stuck his head round the front room door. Sure enough, his dad was fast asleep and snoring in front of the TV. *So far so good*, thought Rory, heading for the porch.

The shoes were lined up as usual. Dad's, Mum's, Callum's and Rory's. But something was wrong. Rory could see that straightaway. There was only one pair of trainers there. One pair was missing. *Callum's* pair! Rory knew because *his* were marked with an 'R' inside, just like all the rest of his shoes and clothes. It was the only way of knowing who's were who's.

So where were they? Where were Callum's trainers? The ones Callum thought were *fine*? Because they wouldn't be fine after Rory had got hold of them, that was for sure! What was it that Mum had said? We couldn't have you running around in trainers with holes in? Well, by the time Rory had finished with them there'd be more hole than actual trainers! His skinflint parents would have no choice. They'd *have* to buy new ones! For *both* of them!

Rory went through to the kitchen. He opened a drawer and took out a big pair of scissors.

Yep, thought Rory. *They should do the trick.*

He tiptoed back upstairs and into the bedroom. Maybe Callum had put his trainers in the wardrobe? He opened the wardrobe door. Nope. No trainers there. *Oh well*, thought Rory. *Maybe they're under the bed?* But when he looked, the trainers weren't there either.

There was a sudden click as Callum switched his bedside light on.

'You looking for these by any chance, Ror?'

'Aaaaaaaaaaaagggggghhhhhhhhh!!!!' screamed Rory.

He looked up to see that Callum had thrown his duvet off. He was wearing his pyjamas. But on closer inspection Rory could see that, on the end of his pyjama-clad legs, Callum was also wearing his trainers. He'd clearly been expecting Rory. Perhaps he really *could* read his brother's mind after all!

'You want to be careful with those scissors,' said Callum. 'You could do some serious damage with those!'

But before Rory could say anything, there was a knock at the door.

'You OK in there, boys?'

'We're fine, Mum,' said Callum.

'Rory just had a bad dream, didn't you, Ror?'

'Yeah,' muttered Rory, glaring at his brother.

Callum may have out-thought him *this* time. But there'd be a next time. *And* a time after *that* if necessary! One thing was certain. Rory would stop at nothing to get those trainers.

***

It had seemed such a good idea at the time. Colouring in his brother's mole with a pink felt tip pen as he slept, then standing in front of the mirror with a brown pen and giving himself one in exactly the same place. But now, with one hand on the kitchen door handle, Rory suddenly didn't feel quite so sure. Would his parents fall for it? *Oh well,* he thought. *Only one way to find out.*

Dad was standing by the sink, making himself a cup of coffee, as Rory walked in.

'Morning, son.'

'Morning, Dad.'

Son, thought Rory. He'd said *son*. But did he know *which* son?

'Is your brother coming down?'

'I think so, Dad, yeah.'

Brother, thought Rory. He'd said *brother*. But *which* brother?

Dad turned around and looked at Rory. Rory allowed himself a quick glance back. He needed some kind of sign. Did Dad think he was Callum or not?

'Mum tells me Rory had a bad dream last night.'

'Yeeessss!!!' said Rory under his breath. His dad *had* fallen for it!

'Pardon?' said Dad.

'Er, yes, Dad. He did,' said Rory, quickly.

It was now or never. Rory knew he had to act quickly before anyone else came in and messed things up.

'Dad?'

'What?'

'Can I have some new trainers, please?'

Dad took a slurp of his coffee.

'But I thought yours were fine.'

'What?' said Rory.

'That's what your mum told me you said. You said the ones you've got were fine.'

'Er, yeah, but I've changed my mind,' said Rory. 'I had another look and they're not actually fine at all. I need some new ones.'

'I see,' said Dad. 'You *need* them, do you?'

'Definitely.'

'Right.'

'So can I, Dad?' said Rory. 'Pleeeeease?'

'Hmmm,' said Dad.

But at that moment the door opened and in walked Mum.

'*Callum* here's changed his mind,' said Dad.

'Oh yeah?' said Mum.

'Yes, apparently he *does* need new trainers after all.'

'Does he now?' said Mum. 'That's interesting.'

She stared at Rory.

'By the look of it, that's not the *only* thing that's changed.'

'What do you mean?' said Rory.

'The mole on your chin's swapped sides,' said Mum. 'It used to be on the right. Now it's on the left.'

'Amazing!' said Dad.

The game was up and Rory knew it.

Mum smiled.

'Nice try, Rory. Next time remember, everything looks back to front in the mirror, OK?'

'OK, Mum,' said Rory, grinning and exposing his chipped front tooth.

The door opened again and in walked the *real* Callum, complete with a very obvious pink dot on his chin where his mole used to be. Mum, Dad and Rory took one look at him and all burst out laughing.

Callum looked puzzled.

'What are you lot looking at?' he said. 'Why are you all laughing at me?'

'You've got something on your chin,' said Rory.

***

'Here you go, Cal,' said Rory.

It was after breakfast. The twins were in their bedroom getting dressed, having first called in at the bathroom to scrub the felt tip from their faces.

'What's this?' said Callum.

'The five pence I owe you,' said Rory. 'We're quits now.'

'No, we're not,' said Callum.

'What do you mean no we're not? Yeah we are! You lent me five pence and now I'm giving it you back!'

'Yeah, but you owe me six pence,' said Callum.

'Six pence?' said Rory. 'How come?'

'One pence interest.'

'What do you mean *one pence interest*? What are you talking about?'

'When you borrow money from a bank and you pay it back, you have to pay a bit extra,' explained Callum. 'And that extra bit is called *interest*.'

'But that's not fair,' said Rory.

'Course it's fair,' said Callum. 'You can't just borrow it for free.'

Rory sighed. His brother might as well have been talking an entirely different language.

'There's a good side to it as well,' said Callum.

'There is?'

Rory didn't look so sure.

'Yeah,' said Callum. 'If *you* save money in your bank account, the bank pays *you* interest!'

'Really?' said Rory, brightening all of a sudden.

'Yeah really,' said Callum. 'And the more money you have in your account, the more interest you get.'

Rory thought about this for a moment.

'Whoa! I had no idea!'

Callum laughed.

'That's because you never have any money in your bank account! Try saving some for a change instead of spending it straightaway!'

But Rory didn't reply. He'd just realised something.

'Oops,' he said.

'What's the matter?' said Callum.

'Does that mean I have to pay Dad interest then?'

'I don't understand,' said Callum. 'Why would you have to pay *Dad* interest?'

Rory grinned.

'Where do you think I got the five pence from?' he said.

Callum looked at his brother.

'Let me get this straight. You borrowed money from *Dad* so that you could pay *me* back?'

Rory shrugged.

'Where else was I supposed to get it?'

There was a knock at the door. Mum and Dad walked in. They didn't look especially happy.

'Your dad and I have been thinking,' said Mum.

'Really?' said Rory, nervously. 'What about?'

'Those trainers you want,' said Mum. 'Sorry. *Need.*'

'Ah, well you see the thing is…' began Rory.

But Mum didn't let him finish.

'If you stop spending all your pocket money the second you get it and actually *save* some for a change. Say £20…'

Mum paused for dramatic effect.

'We'll give you the rest!'

Mum and Dad broke into broad smiles.

'Do you hear that, Rory?' said Dad. 'Not *lend. Give*!'

'We won't even buy Callum an identical pair,' said Mum. 'You can be different for a change!'

'What do you say, son?' said Dad.

It was a good question. What *should* Rory say?

'That's very kind, Mum.'

'Sound fair enough?' said Dad.

'Very fair Dad,' said Rory. 'But…'

'But what, son?'

Rory looked at his parents for a moment.

'I don't actually *want* trainers anymore.'

'What?' said Mum.

'What?' said Dad.

'I've changed my mind,' said Rory. 'I want a skateboard instead!'

'A skateboard?' said Mum.

The twins looked at each other and grinned.

'Copycat,' said Callum.

The Authors

Theresa Breslin

Theresa was born and brought up in a small town in the middle of Scotland close to castles, old burial grounds and the Roman Wall, all of which helped fuel an active imagination as a child, further developed by a love of reading.

While working as a mobile librarian she wrote her first book – the route included a small village where the local steel mill closed down devastating the community. She has been described as an outstanding writer who combines a powerful sense of drama with memorable characters and superb storytelling. She likes writing humorous stories where children cause confusion, and triumph over adult foolishness.

She won the Carnegie Medal for *Whispers in the Graveyard,* her compelling story of a dyslexic boy. Her work is in translation in a number of languages, is used extensively in schools and has been filmed for television and dramatised for radio. She is committed to promoting reading and writing and will talk about this to anyone who will listen!

In her spare time she loves to browse through old children's books and also enjoys walking, films, theatre, reading and exploring old graveyards. She loves to travel and hear stories from countries around the world.

These are just some of Theresa's books which you might like to read:

Whispers in the Graveyard (Mammoth Reprint 2007)

Divided City (Corgi, 2006)

Mutant (Barrington Stoke, 2005)

Starship Rescue (Barrington Stoke, 2005)

Prisoner in Alcatraz (Barrington Stoke, 2006)

The Magic Factory – Trick or Treat (OUP, 2007)

The Magic Factory – Cold Spell (OUP, 2007)

The Magic Factory – Midsummer Magic (OUP, 2007)

The Dream Master Series – 4 books
(Corgi, 2000–2006)

Find out more about Theresa at
www.theresabreslin.co.uk

Alison Prince

Alison Prince is an accomplished artist and respected biographer and poet, as well as one of the top writers for young people. Her life and career have been enviably varied, colourful and successful; from penning those immortal words 'Pugh, Pugh, Barney McGrew...' for the *Trumpton* TV series, to writing a novel with the help of 21 Lincolnshire children (*How's Business*, 1987), to winning the Guardian Children's Fiction Award in 1996 with her contemporary Glaswegian Robin Hood story, *The Sherwood Hero*.

Oranges and Murder, Alison's first novel is a wonderful, atmospheric thriller full of rich period detail and won the Scottish Arts Council Award. Her second novel *Three Blind Eyes* is highly intriguing, with murderous villains.

Alison Prince has also won a scholarship to the Slade School of Fine Art, raised three children, managed a small farm and produced major, highly acclaimed biographies of Kenneth Grahame and Hans Christian Andersen.

Alison lives on the Isle of Arran, Scotland.

These are just some of Alison's books which you might like to read:

Cat Number 3 (Transworld, 1999)

Boojer (Transworld, 2002)

Bumble (Transworld, 2001)

Spud (Transworld, 2003)

How's Business (Hodder, 2002)

The Sherwood Hero (Macmillan, 2002)

Tower Block Pony (Orchard Books, 2004)

Screw Loose (Barrington Stoke, 2002)

The Summer House (Walker, 2004)

Jacoby's Game (Walker, 2006)

Find out more about Alison
at www.alisonprince.co.uk

Nicola Morgan

Nicola Morgan was born and educated in a boys' boarding school and was taught by her parents. She then went to a girls' boarding school, where no one was at all impressed by the tree-climbing and weapon-making skills she had acquired. She went to Cambridge University and studied Classics and Philosophy, before becoming a teacher, later specialising in teaching children with dyslexia; having taught for sixteen years she founded Magic Readers, followed by The Child Literacy Centre, which she still runs.

Nicola has had more than 80 books published, many of which have been UK bestsellers. She is best known for writing for older children and teenagers, and has won two Scottish Arts Council Awards for her teenage fiction, including The Scottish Children's Book of the Year for *Sleepwalking*. She also has a long-standing fascination with the human brain and *Blame My Brain* was shortlisted for the prestigious Aventis Prize.

Nicola is also Chair of the Society of Authors in Scotland, speaks at festivals, conferences and in schools, and writes for the *Guardian, The Scotsman* and *TES*. She lives in Edinburgh with her husband, two daughters and a spoilt Labrador.

These are just some of Nicola's books which you might like to read:

Chicken Friend – 8+ (Walker Books, 2005)

The Highwayman's Footsteps – 10+
(Walker Books, 2006)

The Highwayman's Curse – 10+
(for publication November 2007)

Know Your Brain – 10+
(for publication November 2007)

Mondays are Red – 11+ (Hodder, 2002)

Fleshmarket – 11+ (Hodder, 2003)

Sleepwalking – 12+ (Hodder, 2004)

Blame My Brain – 12+ (Walker Books, 2005)

The Passionflower Massacre – 13+ (Hodder, 2005)

Find out more about Nicola at
www.nicolamorgan.co.uk

Jonathan Meres

I left school at the age of sixteen and joined the merchant navy as a navigating cadet. I spent the next seven years sailing around the world.

I left the sea because I wanted to be a rock star but ended up being an ice cream van driver instead. I went to live in London and put my vast experience in the ice cream industry to use working in the ice cream parlour in Harrods. Then one day I saw an advertisement looking for actors. I went to the audition and got the part. It was a very weird play. It had goats in it. Real goats not pretend ones. Then I got a job with a childrens' theatre company and did that for a couple of years before trying stand up comedy. (We've reached 1984 now.) I was a comedian for about ten years and I won a *Time Out* magazine award for comedy.

I did my last comedy gig in 1994 and since then my job description has been writer/actor, strictly in that order.

These are just some of Jonathan's books which you might like to read:

Somewhere Out There (Random House, 1998)

Yo! Diary! (Piccadilly Press, 1999)

The Big Bad Rumour (Random House, 2000)

Yo! Diary! 2 – And Another Thing
(Piccadilly Press, 2000)

Find out more about Jonathan at
www.jonathanmeres.co.uk

Learning and Teaching Scotland has a remit that actively promotes a climate of innovation, ambition and excellence throughout the Scottish education system. The Scottish Centre for Financial Education (SCFE) as part of Learning and Teaching Scotland takes the view that 'On the Money' helps meet this requirement. Our remit also encourages working with key partners and the partnership that has been established with the authors, teachers involved in the pilot, Standard Life and the Scottish Book Trust has been exciting and dynamic. We are also sure that the approach to developing financial capability in our young people through their engagement with these stories will prove to be very successful.

For further information on Learning and Teaching Scotland visit our website at www.LTScotland.org.uk

Standard Life

At Standard Life we view corporate responsibility as an integral part of managing our day to day business – as important as delivering excellent customer service and growing the business profitably.

We have had a focused community investment policy since 1992 and over this period we have formed strong partnerships with education and the wider community.

The four areas that our education and community activities support reflect our business and values. They are:

Working Life: Helping people develop the core skills and knowledge they need for the important stages in their life.
Financial Life: Supporting education initiatives to help people develop their financial capability.
Healthy Life: Working to enhance and promote healthy living.
Strengthen Life: Supporting the well-being of disadvantaged and vulnerable groups.

Further information is available on our website at www.standardlife.com

pfeg supports the development and choice of suitable and effective material for teaching financial capability to young people, from reception class through to school leavers, through our **pfeg** Quality Mark accreditation system.

We award the Quality Mark to financial education teaching resources that meet the high standards set out in our code of practice. **pfeg** Quality Mark is awarded to resources that:

- are accurate and up-to-date
- match curriculum requirements
- are easily available, adaptable and often free
- cover an appropriate range of financial topics
- have been developed in partnership with teachers and tested in schools